courtney

The Ocean Fairies

D0388723

To Emma Clerkin, a very
special friend of the fairies!

Special thanks
to Sue Mongredien

ORCHARD BOOKS
338 Euston Road, London NW1 3BH
Orchard Books Australia
Level 17/207 Kent Street, Sydney, NSW 2000
A Paperback Original

First published in 2010 by Orchard Books

A CIP catalogue record for this book is available
from the British Library.

ISBN 978 1 40830 821 9

1 3 5 7 9 10 8 6 4 2

Printed in Great Britain

The paper and board used in this paperback are natural recyclable
products made from wood grown in sustainable forests. The
manufacturing processes conform to the environmental regulations
of the country of origin.

Orchard Books is a division of Hachette Children's Books,
an Hachette UK company

www.hachette.co.uk

Courtney
the Clownfish Fairy

by Daisy Meadows

ORCHARD BOOKS

www.rainbowmagic.co.uk

The Fairyland Palace

Fairyland Royal Aquarium

GALA
FAIRYLAND ROYAL AQUARIUM

Kirsty's Gran's House

Lighthouse

The Park

Rockpool

Ocean Star Sailing Ship

Lea-On-Sea

Whales

The Magical Conch Shell at my side,
I'll rule the oceans far and wide!
But my foolish goblins have shattered the shell,
So now I cast my icy spell.

Seven shell fragments, be gone, I say,
To the human world to hide away,
Now the shell is gone, it's plain to see,
The oceans will never have harmony!

Contents

Where's Courtney?   9

Underwater Fun   19

Here Comes Trouble!   29

A Race for the Shell   39

Bouncing Bubbles   49

All Together Now   59

Where's Courtney?

"I can't believe we're going home tomorrow," Rachel Walker said, gazing out to sea. "This has been *such* a brilliant holiday!"

"I know," her best friend Kirsty Tate agreed. "I'll never forget it."

The two girls were standing on the end of Leamouth Pier, leaning against the railings. It was a warm, clear day, and the sun cast dancing sparkles on the water below. Jolly music boomed out from the funfair behind them. Kirsty and Rachel had been staying with Kirsty's gran for a week of the spring holiday, and it had been a very exciting time. They had met the seven Ocean Fairies, and enjoyed some wonderful adventures  with them, trying to find the lost pieces of a Magical Golden Conch Shell.

Rachel sighed. "I'm a bit worried, you know. We still haven't found the last piece of the Conch Shell, and time's running out."

"We can't let the holiday end without finding it," Kirsty replied. "I really hope we meet Courtney the Clownfish Fairy soon!"

Kirsty and Rachel had met the Ocean Fairies on the first day of their holiday, when they'd been invited to a special Ocean Gala Party in Fairyland.

Every year at the party, Shannon the Ocean Fairy played a song on the Magical Golden Conch Shell, which would ensure happy times in and around the oceans for everyone. But this year, before she could play the tune, mean Jack Frost had gatecrashed the party, sneering that he hated the seaside. He didn't like seeing anyone enjoy themselves and loathed getting sand between his toes! He'd ordered his goblin servants to seize the Golden Conch Shell, but unfortunately they'd started squabbling over it, then dropped it.

The shell had smashed into seven pieces, but before the Ocean Fairies could grab them, Jack Frost had used his magic to send the shell pieces out into the human world. Luckily, the Fairy Queen had acted quickly. She'd sent the Ocean Fairies' seven magic creatures – a dolphin, a seal, a penguin, a turtle, a starfish, a whale and a clownfish - out into the human world too, to find and protect each piece of the conch. So far, Kirsty and Rachel had managed to help six of the Ocean Fairies find their magic creatures and the hidden pieces of the Conch Shell, but they hadn't found Courtney's clownfish, or the seventh piece of shell.

And until the shell was put back together, the girls knew there would be chaos throughout the oceans.

The two girls gazed at the funfair rides, hoping they might see the little fairy. There was a helter-skelter, a bouncy castle, a spinning octopus ride, and lots of sideshows. "Is that a sparkle of fairy dust near the helter-skelter?" Kirsty asked, pointing.

Rachel shaded her eyes to see. "No," she replied sadly. "It's just the flash of a camera." She linked an arm through Kirsty's. "It's no good us searching for Courtney,"  she went on. "Remember what Queen Titania says? We shouldn't look for fairy magic, it will find its way to us."

Kirsty nodded. "You're right," she said. "Come on, let's go round the funfair. There's a clown over there, look."

The girls wandered closer to the clown who was dressed in a red-and-white spotty romper suit, a little black hat with a yellow flower on top, huge floppy boots, and full clown make-up. He was bending balloons into shapes, and the girls watched as he turned a red balloon into a dog-shape for a little girl, and a blue balloon into a sword-shape for a boy.

The clown saw them watching and waved. "Hello!" he called. "Let me make you something."

He pulled out a long orange balloon and twisted it deftly into a fish-shape. "Here we are! Don't let him swim away!"

"Thank you," Kirsty said, taking the fish-balloon. Then, as the clown walked away, Kirsty's heart gave a skip of excitement.

There was a magical glimmer coming from inside the balloon…and as she looked closer, she realised it was Courtney the Clownfish Fairy!

Underwater Fun

Courtney waved from inside the balloon, and then, with a little burst of sparkles, magically appeared in front of the girls. She had long, red, wavy hair, held back from her face with a pretty lilac headband.

Her top was patterned with leaf and fish shapes, and she wore it over black leggings. "Hello there," she said, as she hovered in mid-air, her beautiful wings glittering in the sunshine. "I'm glad I found you two. I really need your help."

She landed lightly on Rachel's shoulder, and Rachel smiled as Courtney's wings tickled her neck. "Of course we'll help," Rachel replied. "Let's go somewhere quieter first, shall we? We don't want anyone to see you."

Kirsty and Rachel walked to an area of the pier that was less busy. An elderly couple dozed in deckchairs, arm-in-arm, but nobody else was around.

"That's better," Courtney said, her tiny fairy voice like tinkling bells. "We've got to find Tickle, my clownfish, and the last piece of the Golden Conch Shell. The oceans are still in turmoil, so as soon as we can get the shell back together, Shannon will be able to play the special tune on it, and set everything to rights."

"What are we waiting for?" Kirsty said excitedly. "Let's start looking!"

Courtney grinned. "Just the words I hoped you'd say," she chuckled. She waved her wand at Kirsty, and then at Rachel, and, as bright orange fairy dust tumbled all around them, the girls felt themselves shrinking down, down, down until they were fairies themselves!

Rachel fluttered her wings, loving the way she felt lighter than air now. But oh, the sea breeze sweeping in was quite strong! It was hard to hover in one place with it buffeting her around!

"Now for some magic bubbles…"
Courtney said, and waved her wand
again. Two orange-tinged bubbles
appeared over Kirsty and Rachel's heads,
then vanished with a POP.
Kirsty and Rachel
knew that they
would now
be able to
breathe
underwater.
"And
finally, let's
go to a lovely
tropical part of
the ocean!" Courtney cried,
waving her wand a third time. A stream
of sparkling fairy dust poured from its tip
and swirled all around the three fairies.

Moments later, they were lifted up by a glittering whirlwind that spun them right away from Leamouth Pier, so fast that Rachel and Kirsty could barely see a thing.

When the whirlwind came to a stop, the girls found themselves in warm blue water, right above the seabed. And what on earth was that in front of them?

"It's an underwater funfair!" Kirsty realised in excitement. "Look, there's an octopus ride – with a real-life octopus!"

She giggled as she watched the octopus spin round very fast, with fish and other sea creatures perched precariously on the ends of its tentacles.

"Oh, and look at the baby turtles," Rachel cried. A giant clam was opening and closing nearby, blowing bubbles that a group of baby turtles were bouncing gleefully on. "They've got their very own bouncy castles!"

The girls marvelled at the sights before them. There were sea creatures gathered together from all around the world – from coral reefs to polar seas, and all the oceans in between. Penguins and seals were whizzing around a huge column of rock, just like a helter-skelter. Whales and dolphins flipped and spun, as if they were performing gymnastics. Other creatures seemed to be dancing in front of the flashing lights created by a group of lantern-fish.

"Wow," Kirsty said, unable to take her eyes off the happy animals. "They're all having so much fun!"

"I could stand here all day watching them," Rachel said, feeling mesmerised by the wonderful scene.

Courtney, however, didn't look so happy. "Hmmm," she said. "I'm glad the sea creatures are enjoying themselves, but lots of them shouldn't be in this part of the ocean! The penguins should be nearer the South Pole, the dolphins should be in cooler seas,  and the whales need much deeper waters than this." She frowned. "It's all because the last piece of shell is still missing. We've got to find it – and fast!"

Here Comes Trouble!

Luckily, in the very next moment, Courtney spotted something that put a smile on her face. "There's Tickle!" she cried, pointing at a nearby rock. The rock was covered with purple and red anemones, and there was a whole group of clownfish playing a sort of 'catch-me-if-you-can' game with them. The clownfish would dart into the anemones, and the anemones would try to close their fronds around them before the clownfish zipped out again.

Rachel smiled as she watched them play. The clownfish were so sweet, with their bright orange and white stripes – and they were all giggling as the anemones tried to catch them. Then one of the clownfish spotted Courtney and his face lit up with a huge grin. "Hello! Hello! Oh, I've missed you!" he cried, swimming over at once.

Courtney beamed and threw her arms around him. "I've missed you too," she replied. "But it looks like you've made lots of friends here."

Tickle nodded. "And I've found the piece of Conch Shell," he said proudly. "It's in one of the anemones. Come on, I'll show you."

Tickle began zooming back towards the anemones, and the three fairies were just about to follow when a chill suddenly spread through the ocean. The sea creatures stopped playing and gazed around in surprise. The anemones and clams closed up tightly as if they were scared.

"What's happening?" Kirsty hissed, feeling goosebumps prickle across her arms and legs.

"I don't know," Courtney replied, shivering. "It's usually so warm here. I wonder if a stray iceberg has floated this way because of the Conch Shell being broken, or..."

She stopped speaking as a long, thin shape appeared on the surface of the water above them, completely blocking out the last rays of sunlight.

Everybody stared up at it. For a second, Rachel thought the shape was a massive whale but then she realised it wasn't a living creature at all.

"It's a submarine!" Kirsty realised aloud.

The three fairies and the ocean creatures gazed up at the submarine in silence as it descended towards them.

It was an icy-blue colour, with icicles hanging from its base, and frost-speckled windows. On the side, in large jaggedy letters, was painted 'The Frosty Diver' and Kirsty's stomach lurched as she read the words. The Frosty Diver? Did that mean the submarine had something to do with horrible Jack Frost and his goblins?

"Oh no," Courtney murmured, clearly thinking the same as Kirsty. "Here comes trouble."

The submarine continued to sink
through the water. Finally, it came to
a halt and Kirsty and Rachel heard
its engine switch off. "What's going
to happen now?" Rachel whispered
nervously, her heart thumping. "Should
we hide?" She was scared of Jack Frost.
He could work powerful icy magic, and
was always in a bad temper.

Courtney squeezed her hand. "Let's wait
and see what happens," she said bravely.

The hatch of the submarine flipped open, and the three fairies held their breath. The sea creatures, too, were silent, waiting to see what emerged from the submarine. Then out clambered a goblin, wearing an icy breathing bubble over his head and huge floppy flippers. He was followed by a second goblin, and then a third, and then a fourth…and lots more goblins until there were at least ten of them standing by the submarine.

Kirsty was just starting to let her breath out – surely there couldn't be room for any more goblins in the submarine, could there? – when she saw one last figure climbing out. Even with his bubble helmet on, there was no mistaking the spiky ice crown on his head, or the ferocious look on his face. Jack Frost!

A Race for the Shell

Jack Frost's cold, piercing eyes fell upon the three nervous fairies, and he gave a gloating laugh. "Ahh, so you're here, are you?" he sneered. "I should have known. Well, that doesn't bother me. My goblins and I are going to find the last piece of the Conch Shell before you do, mark my words!"

"No, you won't," Courtney said. "We'll find it first!"

Jack Frost laughed again, the scornful sound ringing out through the water. "I don't think so," he replied. "Goblins! To work! Find that piece of shell or you'll all be in big trouble!"

The goblins leapt to obey their master and began swimming in all directions, searching for the shell. Some peered under bushy seaweed plants, others dug through the sand, while one silly goblin even lifted a seal's flippers to peer underneath them! "Do you mind?" the seal snapped huffily, swimming away with its nose in the air.

Kirsty was expecting Courtney to
make a dive for the anemones but to her
surprise, the fairy stayed still. "Shouldn't
we go and get
the shell?" she
whispered.

Courtney
shook her
head and
leaned over
so that both
girls could
hear her whispered
reply. "Not right now," she said softly.
"Look, Jack Frost's got his beady eyes on
us. If we swim straight for the anemones,
he'll know that the shell piece is there.
And with so many goblins here, we'll be
overpowered within seconds."

"We'll have to try and distract him somehow," Rachel said thoughtfully, watching as one of the goblins tickled a giant clam to make it open up. The goblin peered inside the clam, looking for the piece of conch, only to back away quickly when the clam shell almost  slammed shut on his long nose! She turned back into the conversation. Now she was getting distracted! But maybe that was the answer…

"I've thought of something," she
hissed to Kirsty and Courtney. "What
if we could get the funfair going again?
Remember how we couldn't stop looking
at it, Kirsty? Well, hopefully it would be
the same for the goblins and Jack Frost.
And if they're distracted by all the funfair
goings-on, we can sneak over to the
anemones and find the piece of Golden
Conch!"

"That's a great idea," Courtney said.
She motioned to Tickle to swim over, and
explained the plan to him in a low voice.

"So, Tickle, we need you to swim round and ask all the creatures to start up the funfair again. And please ask them to make it look as exciting as possible!" She grinned. "I'll do my bit to help with some fairy magic, too."

Off went Tickle, zooming through the water like a bright orange streak of light, to spread the word. Slowly, the fair came back to life. The lantern fish began shining their lights once more, the octopus waggled its tentacles inviting creatures back on for a ride, and the seals started whizzing down the rocky helter-skelter again.

"Let's see what else we can add…"
Courtney said, waving her wand in a
complicated pattern. Orange fairy dust
swirled from its tip, and up sprang what
looked like a coconut shy, with large
white shells instead of coconuts. There
was also a 'Tug of War' stall with a
thick rope of seaweed to pull, and a
'Test Your Strength' tower, with a huge
rock to lift up.

"Oooohhh!" the goblins chorused as they noticed what was happening. "How cool is this?" one cheered, running to try the shell game.

"Brilliant!" another whooped, sprinting to the helter-skelter. "Woo-hoo!" he squealed as he whizzed down it. "Come on, boys, have a go!"

With all the goblins abandoning the shell-search, the fairies were able to swim over to the anemones where Tickle had said the shell was hidden.

Tickle was still busily passing on the message about the funfair, so he wasn't there to tell them exactly which anemone the shell was hidden in. "Let's look through them all," Kirsty suggested, gently opening the soft pink fronds of the anemone nearest to her. "No, it's not in this one…"

The fairies worked swiftly, checking through the anemones' fronds as fast as they could. But after only a few moments, they heard a triumphant shout from Jack Frost. "Aha! So that's where the shell is – hidden in the anemones, eh? Move over, fairies. I'm going to find that shell first. Just watch me!"

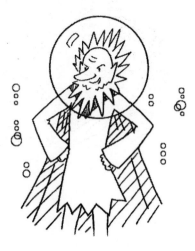

Bouncing Bubbles

As Jack Frost strode along the seabed towards them, Rachel felt her spirits plunge. Oh, no! Just what they didn't want to happen!

49

Courtney, however, wasn't about to give up without a fight. She waved a wand, sending a shower of sparkles whirling towards Jack Frost. The glittering sparkles circled some giant clams near him which then blew out bubbles... only these weren't ordinary bubbles.

They were enormous, magical bubbles – so big that they knocked Jack Frost off his feet and bounced him away! Jack Frost furiously tried to pop the bubbles with his wand, but the magic held fast. Boing!

Boing! Boing! Rachel and Kirsty couldn't help giggling as he was bounced away. He even started to look a little bit seasick with the bouncing motion!

"Brilliant, Courtney," laughed Rachel. "Now to find that piece of the Conch Shell!"

With Jack Frost out of the way, the water began to feel warmer, and the anemones started opening and closing again. Tickle swam over, and Courtney hugged him. "Just in time! Can you tell us which anemone has the hidden piece of the Conch Shell?" she asked.

Tickle pointed a fin. "That one… I think," he said. "Or is it this one? Or maybe it's one of those… Oh, I can't remember!"

Then the fairies heard a series of muffled pops – and turned to see a furious-looking Jack Frost shaking his fist at them in the distance. "He's managed to burst the bubbles," Kirsty realised in dread.

"And now he's heading this way – quick, guys! We've got to find that shell right NOW!"

Just as Rachel was starting to despair, she suddenly noticed the frond tips of one sea anemone were sparkling faintly. Could that be because of the Conch Shell?

She swam over to look, her heart thumping. When the anemone opened up again, she dipped her hand inside…and her fingers closed around something hard and smooth. The seventh piece of the Magical Golden Conch Shell!

She drew it out, feeling a huge surge
of relief. "I've got it!" she called to Kirsty
and Courtney. "I've found it!"

"Oh, well done!" Courtney cried, her
eyes bright with happiness. "Brilliant,
Rachel!"

An angry shout came from Jack Frost
as he saw the shining piece of shell in
Rachel's hand. He was closing in on
them, and raised his wand, glaring.

Whizz! An icy bolt of magic sped
through the water from Jack Frost's wand
and hit the piece of shell with a smack,
immediately encasing it in ice.

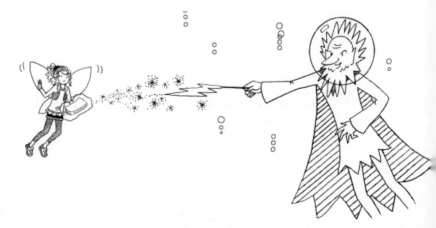

"Ow!" Rachel cried, her hand stinging from the freezing cold. Before she knew what she was doing, she had dropped the piece of shell…and an icy hand stretched forward and snatched it.

"I'll have that, thank you very much!" snapped Jack Frost.

"Oh no you won't!" cried brave little Tickle. He flapped a flipper as if  beckoning his friends, and then a whole group of clownfish launched themselves at Jack Frost.

Jack Frost looked taken aback at
this orange-and-white army that had
appeared from out of nowhere – and
then, as the clownfish began to tickle him
all over, he let out a surprised giggle.

Rachel and Kirsty stared in amazement
as the clownfish flipped their ticklish
flippers and tails behind Jack
Frost's knees, under his
chin and around
his ears. Some
even swam down
to tickle his toes.
The two friends had
never seen their old
enemy laugh so much,
and it was quite something to
see him squirming helplessly from all
the tickling.

"Ooh! Ah ha ha ha! Hoo-hoo-hoo!
Stop! Oh, ho ho ho, stop!" he wailed,
trying and failing to get the fish away
from him. Before long, he was completely
weak with laughter and try as he might
to cling on to the piece of ice
which contained the shell,
he lost his grip on it
when the clownfish
began tickling
his tummy. To
their great
excitement, the
fairies saw the
ice piece drop
from his fingers,
and all of them
swooped to catch it.
This was their chance!

57

All Together Now

Kirsty got to the ice ball first and grabbed it – but it was still so freezing cold, she couldn't bear to hold onto it.

Luckily, Courtney was able to use her magic to melt the ice around the fragment of shell, and to transform it to its Fairyland size.

"We've done it!" Courtney cried happily, hugging Rachel and Kirsty, whilst keeping a tight hold on the shell. "Come on, Tickle, you can leave him alone now. We're going back to Fairyland!"

Tickle swam over to his fairy mistress who gave him a big kiss, then shrank him back down to his Fairyland size. Jack Frost, meanwhile, could only scowl, knowing he was beaten.

"Never mind, Your Frostiness," one of the goblins called to him sympathetically, "Come and have a go on the helter-skelter. It's really fun!"

Jack Frost pulled a face. "Fun? I thought I'd told you, nothing about the sea is fun in my opinion. Although…" His eyes widened as he saw the octopus ride whizzing around, with its eight passengers all squealing with excitement. "I suppose that might be…enjoyable."

As he hurried off to join the goblins, Rachel was sure she saw an eager light in his eyes, and smiled to herself.

Maybe Jack Frost was about to find out that the ocean was a fun place, after all!

Then Courtney waved her wand, whizzing all three fairies and Tickle to Fairyland in another sparkling whirlwind.

As the whirlwind cleared, and they landed gently on the ground, Kirsty and Rachel saw that they were back in the majestic hall of the Fairyland Royal Aquarium. Tickle was back in his fish tank, and King Oberon, Queen Titania, Shannon the Ocean Fairy and the other six Ocean Fairies were gathered, as if they'd been waiting for Courtney, Kirsty and Rachel's return.

When the crowd of fairies saw the golden piece of the Conch Shell in Courtney's hands, a great cheer went up from everyone – and the six ocean creatures all swam about excitedly in their tanks as they saw that their friend Tickle was safely back in Fairyland, too.

Shannon rushed over, her eyes shining with happiness. "You found it! Well done, all of you!"

She took the shell-piece gently from Courtney, then took it to where the other six pieces had been put together.

She fitted the last piece carefully in place and there was a flurry of golden sparkles. Then all seven fragments of the shell were magically joined together, as if the shell had never been broken.

With a big smile, Shannon raised the Conch Shell to her lips and played a lilting melody that sent shivers down Rachel and Kirsty's spines.

The hall was hushed as everyone listened, but once she had finished, another cheer went up, and all the fairies burst into applause.

"So everything in the oceans will now be back as it should," Shannon said, beaming proudly. "Thanks to the Ocean Fairies, and our very special helpers!"

Kirsty and Rachel blushed with pride. "We enjoyed every minute of it," Kirsty said.

"I'm glad to hear it," the queen said. "And we'd like to thank you for your help with a little gift."

"We hope they'll remind you of your ocean adventures," King Oberon said, smiling as he gave each of the girls a present, wrapped in gold paper and tied with a blue ribbon.

Kirsty and Rachel unwrapped the presents to find that they'd each been given a smaller version of the Magical Golden Conch Shell. "It's beautiful, thank you!" Rachel cried, gazing at the shiny, sparkling shell in her hands.

Queen Titania smiled. "Whenever you raise the shell to your ear, you'll be able to hear Shannon's special song," she said. "That way you'll never forget how you helped us once again."

"Thank you. We love helping our fairy friends," Kirsty said, holding the shell to her ear and listening to the beautiful tune.

"Well, we love being friends with you," Queen Titania replied, "although I'm sad to say it's time for you to return to your own world now. We hope we'll see you again very soon!"

The girls hugged all their fairy friends goodbye, and then Queen Titania threw a handful of sparkling fairy dust over them. The glittering whirlwind appeared for one last time and took them back to where they'd been standing on Leamouth Pier when the adventure had begun. They were girls again, with their beautiful fairy wings gone, but they still had their lovely shell gifts in their hands.

"There you are!" came a voice, and Rachel and Kirsty turned to see Kirsty's gran bustling along the pier towards them. "I can't believe our week together is almost over. I hope you haven't been too bored staying here with me."

"Bored? Not a bit!" Kirsty said. "We've had a brilliant time here."

"I've loved staying with you by the seaside," Rachel added.

Splash! As the three of them gazed out to sea, a pod of dolphins suddenly leapt from the water, making them all jump.

"Well! Now there's a treat for your last day here," Kirsty's gran said happily. "It's not every day that you see dolphins, is it?"

Kirsty and Rachel shared a secret smile as they watched the playful dolphins. They'd seen whales, penguins, octopuses, seals…all sorts of amazing sea creatures while they'd been on holiday in Leamouth. But it probably wasn't a good idea to tell Kirsty's gran that. "The ocean is a magical place," Kirsty replied instead, gazing out at the water happily. "A truly magical place!"

The Ocean Fairies have found all the
pieces of the Magical Golden Conch
Shell! Now Rachel and Kirsty
must help...

Belle the Birthday Fairy

Parties in Peril!

"I can't wait to see Mum's face when she arrives at her surprise birthday party!" Rachel Walker said with a little skip of excitement.

"Yes, she'll be so amazed when she realises that you and your dad have arranged it all!" replied her best friend Kirsty Tate, swinging her rollerskates.

Kirsty was staying at Rachel's house in Tippington for the half term holiday. Rachel's mum thought that Kirsty was just visiting for a holiday, but she was also there to attend Mrs Walker's surprise party!

"Everything's ready," said Rachel, counting the list off on her fingers. "The food, the music, the decorations for the village hall..."

"What about the cake?" Kirsty asked.

"Dad's ordered that from the baker's," said Rachel with a smile. "He's not very good at baking and he wanted it to be perfect!"

The friends were on their way to the local park to go rollerskating. As they passed the village hall where Mrs Walker's party was to be held, Rachel squeezed Kirsty's hand.

"Let's just quickly look inside," she said. "I want to show you where I'm planning to put all the decorations on the day of the party."

"Ooh, yes!" said Kirsty eagerly. "I'm

really looking forward to helping you decorate the hall and lay out the food."

They put their heads around the door and their mouths fell open in astonishment. A group of boys and girls were there in their best party outfits, but no one seemed to be having a good time. The guests were talking in low voices and they all looked upset. Some of the parents were kneeling on the floor, clearing up squashed cakes and spilled party snacks. A box of decorations sat untouched by the window. There was a stereo near the stage, but it was making a strange, whining sound and there was smoke coming out of it.

A little girl was standing by the door with her head hanging down. She was wearing a pretty pink dress with a white sash, but she looked very sad.

"Hello," said Rachel. "Is this your party?"

The little girl nodded her head and her big blue eyes filled up with tears.

"Everything's gone wrong!" she sobbed. "Half my guests didn't remember it's my birthday today and didn't turn up. The food tables collapsed and squashed my birthday cake. None of the decorations would stay up on the walls. Now the stereo has broken so we can't even do any dancing."

Kirsty put her arm around the little girl's shaking shoulders. She didn't know what to say. The girl's mum hurried over to them.

"I'm sorry, Maya, but Dad can't mend the stereo. We're going to have to have the party at home."

"But we can't fit everyone into our house," said Maya, looking miserable.

"I know, but we have no choice," said her mum sadly. "You'll have to pick ten friends to bring with you. Everyone else will just have to go home."

Trying not to cry, Maya walked off with her mum. Rachel and Kirsty left the hall and carried on towards the park.

"I feel so sorry for Maya," said Rachel. "It's really unlucky that all those things went wrong."

They arrived in the park and sat down to put on their rollerskates. They both felt upset about the little girl's birthday being ruined.

"If only one of the Party Fairies had been here," Kirsty said with a sigh. "I'm sure they could have helped."

Rachel and Kirsty were good friends with the fairies, and had often helped them to outwit bad-tempered Jack Frost and his naughty goblin servants...

Read the rest of

Belle the Birthday Fairy

to find out what magic happens next...

(available May 2009)

The Ocean Fairies

Win Rainbow Magic goodies!

In every book in the Ocean Fairies series
(books 85-91) there is a hidden picture of a shell with a
letter in it. Find all seven letters and re-arrange them to
make a special Ocean Fairies word, then send it to us.
Each month we will put the entries into a draw and select
one winner to receive a Rainbow Magic sparkly T-shirt
and goody bag!

Send your entry on a postcard to Rainbow Magic Ocean
Fairies Competition, Orchard Books, 338 Euston Road,
London NW1 3BH. Australian readers should write to
Hachette Children's Books, Level 17/207 Kent Street,
Sydney, NSW 2000.
New Zealand readers should write to Rainbow Magic
Competition, 4 Whetu Place, Mairangi Bay, Auckland,
NZ. Don't forget to include your name and address.
Only one entry per child.
Final draw: 30th April 2011.

Have you checked out the

website at:

www.rainbowmagic.co.uk

Meet the Twilight Fairies

in September 2010!

Ava the Sunset Fairy
978-1-40830-906-3

Lexi the Firefly Fairy
978-1-40830-907-0

Zara the Starlight Fairy
978-1-40830-908-7

Morgan the Midnight Fairy
978-1-40830-909-4

Yasmin the Night Owl Fairy
978-1-40830-910-0

Maisie the Moonbeam Fairy
978-1-40830-911-7

Sabrina the Sweet Dreams Fairy
978-1-40830-912-4